# TOO BIG

# HOLLY KELLER

GREENWILLOW BOOKS · New York

Greenwillow Books. a division of
William Morrow & Company. Inc..
105 Madison Avenue. New York. N.Y. 10016.
Printed in the United States of America
First Edition    10 9 8 7 6 5 4 3 2 1

Library of Congress Cataloging in Publication Data

Keller. Holly.   Too big.
Summary: When his new brother comes home
from the hospital. Henry discovers he's too
big for some of the things he'd like to do.
[1. Babies—Fiction.
2. Brothers and sisters—Fiction.
3. Opossums—Fiction] I. Title.
PZ7.K28132To 1983    [E]    82-15653
ISBN 0-688-01998-6
ISBN 0-688-01999-4 (lib. bdg.)

FOR MY VERY SMALL FRIEND
KATIE

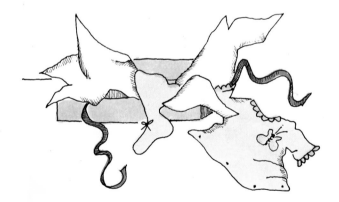

"You will be Mama's big boy now,"
Papa told Henry before he left to
bring Mama and Baby Jake home from
the hospital.

Henry and Auntie waited together.

Jake was small enough to fit in a basket
next to Mama's bed.

"I'll keep Jake company," Henry said.

"No, no, Henry." Mama laughed.
"You're too big."

Auntie helped Mama fix Jake's bottles.
Henry filled one with chocolate milk.
"This one is for me."

"Silly Henry," Auntie said. "You're too big."

Then Papa put Jake on the bed
to change his diaper.
"Me next," Henry said. And he
giggled.
"Scoot, young man," Papa said.
"You are too big."

Auntie told Henry it was time
for Jake to sleep.

Henry played a lullaby on his drum.
"You are too big for that," Mama scolded.
And she sent Henry to his room.

Henry watched the birds in the nest outside his window.

The mailman came down the path and
waved hello. He had a package for Jake.

"Don't ring the doorbell," Henry whispered.
"Jake is sleeping."

Henry tiptoed to the door.

"Henry," Mama called. "You can come out now. Grandpa is here."

Henry came into the living room.

Papa tried not to smile, but he couldn't help it. Then Mama smiled. Auntie chuckled, and Grandpa laughed out loud. Henry pulled off Jake's bonnet. Then he laughed too.

"I'm too big!"

"You <u>are</u> big, Henry," said Grandpa.

"But not too big for this, I hope."

"And nobody is too big for this," Mama
said. And she gave Henry a great big hug.